Dodging Karma

By Mariah Carson

ISBN - **978-1-105-87103-0**

Printing by Lulu Press.

Dedication

To my parents Andrea & Charles Carson that has always supported me, loved me and showed me that anything is possible as long as I am dedicated, & have the passion to succeed. That has always stuck with me & made me into the young author I am today. To my fiancé Robert who supports me, console me and gives me the drive to keep going & the determination to keep striving for excellence. To my grandmother who is the strongest women that I know, which ultimately made me into the strongest women I am today. Finally, to my loving family that I couldn't and wouldn't be who I am without all the fighting, loving, and passion that we all show one another each and every day. I love you all and I dedicate my success to all of you.

Jonah

Staring in her big brown eyes, I always knew she was the one for me. Looking at her made me hot, made me want to lose control. I became aroused. I tried to get my mind off the naughty images that were surfacing. I started thinking of water. Laying on a beach, relaxing, listening to the waves roar. Her laying on my chest, me grabbing every inch of her body that I could reach. Feeling her body on mine as the sun beamed on her smooth, vivacious skin. It was no use. My mind reverted right back to reality. I couldn't help myself. I wanted her, needed her. I picked her up, making the pink boy shorts she was wearing inch further and further up her thighs, hugging every part of her skin like a glove. I grabbed her, pulled her closer to me. I ripped into her like a Jack rabbit, trying to make her feel and crave every inch of me.

"Oooouuu… Ahhhhhh…Yessssss!" Neveah screamed as the sensation intensified. I drove deeper and faster inside her. She dug her nails in my back as I caressed her inner thighs with soft kisses. We had been in this fuck fest nonstop for the past 3 hours. Neveah was beautiful. She was 5'4", caramel complexion, nice full lips with a big ole ghetto booty to match. She was super intelligent with a Masters in Psychiatry. She was book smart with a dash of crazy, and just enough hood to keep you intrigued. She had all the qualities I looked for in a lady. She was every man’s dream, but I was lucky enough to call her my wife of 2 1/2 years.

The first day I met Neveah, I knew she was the queen for me. I was standing in Juicy Crab with my boy Danny from the neighborhood. Danny was picking up some dinner for his baby mama and 4-year-old daughter before we went to Magic City with the fellas for some much needed time away. There she was, sitting at the table across from us, with her back turned to me. Even though I was not facing her, I could tell she was a beauty.

I walked up to her as she talked to the older, but just as beautiful woman sitting across from her. “Hey pretty ladies," I said, stopping them in mid-conversation. "Hello," they said in sync. "My name is Jonah, but everyone calls me Jay." "Nice to meet you, Jay," the older lady said with a huff. "Can we help you?" the other voice asked. "Not to sound crazy or anything, but I came over here hoping to ask this beautiful lady for her number," I said, looking down at the beauty sitting with her back to me. Without saying another word, she handed me a napkin with numbers on it and returned to her conversation with the older beauty. I took that as my cue to leave, so I turned around and kept it moving.

That was the first day of our beautiful journey together. Neveah walked into the bathroom. "Baby, I'm starving" I she said. "Let's go to breakfast. I'm about to hop in the shower and get ready. Come join me." I did as I was told.

We made love a few times more, got dressed and grabbed brunch at IHOP. We ate our food and then said our goodbyes. We both were already late for work.

Being a club owner at the hottest adult entertainment club in Southside of Compton had its perks. I walked into the building to see Julia standing there waving her hand, trying to get my attention. I was not trying to deal with her bullshit this early afternoon, so I walked right past her.

“Where the hell have you been? I've been calling you!” Julia yelled. I was annoyed and snapped. “Not that it's any of your business, but me and MY WIFE slept in and went for breakfast this morning!” I yelled with an attitude. “The hell it’s not my business!” Julia continued. “It became my business six months ago when you started fucking me! It became my business when you put a baby in me.” Julia sobbed. “Wait, what damn baby?” Julia’s ranting finally began to phase me.

I grabbed her arm and pulled her into the nearest vacant room. “Yes, I'm pregnant Jonah. I've been trying to figure out how to tell you. I am six weeks along.” Julia smiled. At that moment I saw nothing but red. I grabbed Julia by the hair and slammed her into the wall. This fantasy had gone on longer than I anticipated. Sex was so easy that I got caught up in the hype. “Bitch, if you ever think about checking me or my whereabouts again, I will fuckin kill you! This baby isn’t mine and even if it is mine, I love my wife! We will never be! You a whore, the whore who left her husband for a mere fantasy!”

I took out a few bills and fired them in her direction. “Get that fixed, because having a baby isn’t an option!” I spat. Losing Neveah wasn’t an option for me. I cheated time and time again with some of the local thots on my payroll, but they meant nothing to me. Neveah was my queen, and outside of cheating, I treated her as such.

“Fuck you, Jonah! I'm having my baby!” Julia screamed, bringing me back to reality. “If you didn’t want this to happen, then you should’ve been more careful and pulled out.”

“Keeping that baby will be the end of you! You won’t have no job, no money, no baby daddy. So, you choose Bitch!" I shouted as I headed to my office. Julia continued to bark and scream, but I didn't care to stop and listen. I needed a drink to think about the club and the even bigger shit hole I got myself into now that Julia was pregnant.

Neveah

After that good dick I just got, I was on Cloud 9. I got in the car, and cranked up the radio as Tank's song, "When We," played.

I got so wrapped up in the song and my thoughts that I didn't notice the light turn red. I did notice the police turn the corner, turned on his sirens, and that I didn't even have my damn seat belt on. As I rushed to fasten it, the police sped by and jumped in front of me, causing me to slam on the brakes. Had I been going any faster, I would have rear-ended the police car. As the officer exited his vehicle, I took my 45 out of my Holster and placed it under the seat.

"Good evening, officer," I said sarcastically. "Did you not see that red light?" he asked. "The light changed just as I was going over the intersection, so I had no other choice." "Get out of the car with your hands up," he said. I did as I was told, holding my license and registration. The officer grabbed both from me and headed to his car.

Five minutes later, he returned with a strange look on his face. I looked towards his car and shook my head when I saw a familiar face duck from the window. A face I thought I'd never see again. "Neveah, you a long way from Houston," he said smirking as he walked towards me. I wasn't interested in responding or even looking his way, so I tried to get into my car to leave. But he grabbed me before I could enter, causing my door to slam unintentionally.

"You thought you could just leave the city and I wouldn't find you?" I glanced away. "Next time don't run a red light. Now, since I'm a nice guy, I will let you off with a warning. But only if you allow me to take you to lunch."

I felt harassed and annoyed. “No thanks!” I snapped and hopped into my car.

Happy to escape the situation, I hauled ass and arrived work in the nick of time. Still in shock over what just happened I couldn’t wait to get to the office. As I walked into the office, I saw my assistant prepping my 3pm appointment. “Good morning Ms. Jenkins,” she said as I made my way into my office to get my mind right before my client walked in. *Knock knock knock.*

“Come in. How may I help you?”

“Hi Ms. Jenkins, your 3pm is ready.”

“Thanks Jazmine, send them in.”

A few seconds later a small petite framed woman with a beautiful smile walked in and greeted me with a firm handshake, followed by a slick eye roll.

“Hi, my name is Julia Strong, and I am so glad you had an opening at such a short notice.”

“Yes, no problem, I had a cancellation at the last minute, so we were able to squeeze you in. Have a seat and we will get started. So, tell me what brings you in here today Julia?”

“Well, I have a lot of things I'm dealing with in my life right now, they are starting to weigh on me and affecting my everyday life. My work life is long, and my hours are even longer,” Julia said. “On top of that, I just found out I am six weeks pregnant by a man that doesn’t want me or anything to do with our baby. I am married, been married for seven years to a wonderful man that loves me to his core, but my husband isn’t my baby's father. I was happily married for a while. It wasn’t until a year ago when I got this new job, that I started o question my life and lose myself in the mix. Four months into my new job, my boss started making advances towards me. One long night we were working late, and one thing led to another. That night I broke all my vows to my husband,” Julia said sadly.

“Every day after that me and my boss have been playing house. I eventually stopped going home for days at a time, sending my husband to voicemail when he called and dodging him at work when he came by. It had gotten so bad that he stopped coming by and the calls stopped as well.

“I was starting to fall in love with my boss, so I didn’t care how it affected my marriage. My boss made all these promises of leaving his wife and starting a new life with me. It wasn’t until today that I realized all of that was a lie, and I had lost my husband for a man that didn’t give a damn about me,” Julia fought back the tears. I stood up and grabbed the tissue off my desk, handing it to her.

“Julia, I want to start off by saying congratulations on the baby, bringing a baby into the world is such a beautiful thing. I also want to say that I am sorry for what you are going through. It is not your fault you fell in love with empty promises and as a result, lost your marriage.

"Let's talk a little more about why you didn't want to talk with your husband. Did you not think he had the right to know what was going on?"

"Yes, I wanted to talk to him, but didn't know what to say," Julia said with fear in her eyes.
"Tell me how that made you feel, Julia, to have a good man that you loved dearly, calling and coming by while you dodged him for weeks. How did that make you feel?"

"I hated every minute of it!" Julia cried. "I hated seeing him call and leave voicemails begging me to come home or texting me asking me to just talk to him. It broke my heart seeing him come up to the job three and four times a week looking for me. I was just too wrapped up in Jonah to think straight."

As Julia said his name, she looked up at me. At that moment, my heart skipped a beat. I didn't want to seem bothered, so I stayed calm.

“Jonah, is that your husband’s name?”

“No, Jonah is my boss that I'm in love with and pregnant by,” Julia smiled mischievously.

I knew deep down this wasn’t going to end pretty, but I remained relaxed.

“Jonah is your boss. Where do you work?” I asked still trying to get all the facts before jumping to conclusions.

Julia blurted out a hysterical laugh that filled the room. With a confused look she sat up and said, “Bitch, how much clearer do you need me to say that I'm fucking your husband and he got me pregnant?!”

My soul dropped. At that moment I couldn't move. I remained quiet looking for answers in her eyes that would indicate she was lying. She began to cry, and I could feel the pain in her soul.
“Your husband has been screwing me for the past six months, selling me all these

dreams of running away together, making a family, and building an empire together. When I found out I was pregnant I was over the moon, and thought this would be a start of our life together. When I told him about the baby this morning, he laughed in my face and told me that he would never leave you and to end this pregnancy!" Julia snapped.

I couldn't move, couldn't speak. I was in total disbelief that this woman came into my place of business with the audacity of telling me about my husband. Telling me my husband has been cheating on me, and to make matters worse has a baby on the way.

I saw red at this point. I remember slapping Julia and choking her. As she screamed my assistant ran in the room trying to get me off of her. Someone must have alerted security because they ran in. I motioned for them to escort her off the premises.

I couldn't believe how my enjoyable day was turning into the worst day of my life. In a matter of 30 minutes, I learned that my husband was not so great after all. I had my assistant cancel all remaining appointments for the day. I couldn't sit on this information I just learned, I had to go see how true it was.

I headed over to Truth, Jonah's nightclub. When I arrived, I didn't speak I just walked straight back to his office and opened the door. To my surprise my husband was sitting at his desk with his head back on the chair. He didn't even realize the door had opened.

"Ahhhhh ahhhh! Keisha don't stop!" he moaned.
"Jonah! What the fuck is this?!" I screamed. Jonah's eyes bucked as they met mine. With tears streaming down my face, I turned around and ran for the nearest exit. Jonah was right behind me begging me to stop and talk about what I just witnessed. I wasn't interested in anything he had to say, I continued to walk quickly until I reached my candy apple red 2019 Audi A7. I grabbed for my keys but was stopped in my tracks

when I felt Jonah tugging at my arm for me to turn around.

“LET ME GO JONAH! I have nothing to say to you!” I screamed. “Go back and let that nasty bitch finish giving you top! Hope it's worth it because what we had is OVER! I WANT A DIVORCE!” I yelled. I managed to push him out of the way, got in the car and sped off.

Jonah

I couldn't believe how selfish Neveah was being. I have been calling her for over an hour now, trying to explain. This shit is beyond me. Why was she even over at the club in the middle of the afternoon? She had clients lined up till 8 tonight. I thought long and hard. As I walked back into Truth trying to wrap my head around the situation I just got myself into, I noticed that Julia was not at her desk.

“Has anyone seen Julia?” I asked around. No one replied, so I went back to the office to grab my phone so I could call her. Julia was gone and not answering her phone. Something isn't adding up. Neveah wouldn't just pop up without calling, and Julia is normally here until 6pm. I called Julia again but no answer. I sent her a text that read, *Julia why aren't you at the club?* Ten minutes later my phone rang. "This is Jonah," I answered knowing exactly who it was.

"I told her everything. Now that your marriage is over, we can finally be together and have our happily ever after like you promised," Julia said calmly.

I was pressed for words, nothing came out. I was on the verge of a mental breakdown. I was about to lose everything I built in just six hours.

"Bitch if you think I would ever claim you or that bastard child you are sadly mistaken, I love my wife! You were just a fuck, an easy one at that. I have an addiction, and you helped me feed the urge while I was working. I went home and made love to my wife EVERY night I said angrily. I will never be with you!" I slammed down the phone.

Unable to manage my anger I threw my phone and it bounced off the wall cracking into pieces. My assistant ran in my office. "Is everything okay boss?"

"Yes, everything is fine. I could use you in about 20 minutes though. Meet me back here to discuss my meetings tomorrow."

"Sure thing."

Thirty minutes passed, and I was still annoyed at how my wife stormed off and even more annoyed at how we left things. Kimberly entered after about three knocks with no response from me. "Hi, Mr. Simmons, you wanted to see me? Sorry it took me longer than anticipated. I got swamped with calls and other things," she said.

I stood up, walked over, and shut the door. Kimberly sat down on the white leather sofa

located next to the window as I poured myself a glass of scotch.
“Mr. Simmons, tomorrow you have a busy day. You have a call at noon with J&R Associates to discuss the license you’ve been waiting for. At 3:00 pm you have an early dinner meeting with Mr. James over at Pelican Diner on MLK. Finally, at 6:00 pm you have a new hire arriving. I could onboard her if you want, but I know how firm you are about training new hires yourself,” Kimberly chuckled.

I ignored her laugh, took the notepad out of her hand, and started rubbing up her thighs, opening her legs until I reached her pearl. A soft moan gasped out of her mouth letting me know she wasn’t offended. I dug deeper and flickered her clit until I felt moisture. I laid her back, opened her legs, and pushed my face deep inside her juices. “Aww! Yesss… Daddy!!” she screamed and moaned as I made love to her love box with my tongue.

She squirmed and pushed her juices further in my mouth. I instantly got turned on as she pulled my dreads and forced my tongue further and deeper inside of her. I came up and began to suck her hard nipples as I went up and down on my shaft, making my hard on even harder.

She sat up and began to undress as I laid there, admiring all the beauty in front of me. She certainly was beautiful. She was 5'2", smooth honey brown skin, nice round areolas with the perfect juicy booty to match. She removed the lace red dress that fitted her body like a glove, removed her white lace thong, and then her white lace bra. She stood completely nude in front of me with only her red heels. I motioned for her to spin around for me, and she obliged. She dropped to her knees and crawled over to me slowly. The anticipation made my Peter jump like he had a mind of his own. She grabbed my Peter and seductively slid her mouth up and down at a slow pace.

"Mmmm…Mmmm…" I moaned in ecstasy. Only my wife could make me moan this loud. Only my wife made me this hard. I've been with a lot of women in my time but not a lot of them made me want them. Most of them were easy lays that cured my huge sexual appetite, but Kimberly was different. She has always been strictly professional with me, even when I did petty things to get her attention, she never acted on it until today.

She looked so good today; I couldn't resist. As she slurped every inch of my hard on, I enjoyed every moment of it. “Damn Ma, you about to make me spill all over those juicy lips,” I said. Kimberly stood up and started dancing on my dick as she rode it at the same time. I was so in love with the things she was doing to me. This feeling I never felt was coming over me.

Kimberly got on all fours, laid over the couch and begin to play with her kitty from the back, I leaned down and started sucking her clit and jerking myself in full force. She moaned and jerked and bounced but I didn’t let up. I kept my tongue going at a steady circular rotation that had her going all kinds of crazy. As I felt her at the brink of bursting all over my face, she jumped up and threw me down and started to ride me backwards. I was in full ecstasy as she rode me all the way to climax. “Ahhhhhhhhh!” I moaned louder than I expected.

At that moment I realized, not only had I cheated again but I enjoyed it. She got up and put her clothes back on. “Well, Mr. Simmons, that was more than I bargained for. But I definitely appreciate you making time for us to go over your schedule for tomorrow,” she walked out trying to play off the amazing sex we just experienced.

Neveah

I am livid I cannot believe what just happened! I slammed on the breaks as I approached a red light. I turned the radio up. To my surprise our wedding song was playing by Major, "This Is Why I Love You."

Tears started streaming down my face. I couldn't believe I was going through this. The sound of my phone ringing startled me, and the ringtone frustrated me even more because it was a ringtone for the same song.

It was Jonah calling and he had been blowing me up since I left. Not only did he cheat on me with a baby on the way, but when I went to confront him, he was getting oral sex from a work thotty.

Bammmmmmm!! I was so wrapped up in my feelings that I didn't see the car trying to drive around me. I stepped out the car frazzled. "I'm so sorry, I didn't even see you. Is everyone okay?" "Yes, we are fine beautiful. Thanks for asking," a deep voice responded.

After examining the damage on both cars, we decided not to call the police and to pay for the damages ourselves since the damages were minor and wouldn't cost much.

"It was fate we met today." He said with a smile. "Can I get your number and maybe take you out some time?" First, I resisted, but after thinking about the day I had, I jumped at the idea. "I am having the worst day and would love to get a drink right now if you want to join me," I replied with a smile.

We took the next exit and arrived at Joe's Bar and Cafe. We were seated at a booth in the back. I ordered a Sex on the Beach, and he ordered a Hennessy with Coke. "I'm out having a drink with a stranger. I don't even know your name," I chuckled.

"My name is Chance and I'm a Taurus," he giggled.

“Hi Chance. I'm Neveah and I'm a Virgo.” We shook hands jokingly. I could feel the sexual tension rising.

We placed our orders, and as we waited, I felt the vibration of the speakers as the music bumped so loud, we could barely hear one another. We finished eating and he paid the tab. We walked to the car and as we began to say our goodbyes something came over me, I felt all this heat rushing in my lower region.

I leaned in and kissed Chance’s lips. I wanted him and I wanted him now! I opened my car door and threw my purse and jacket in. I lifted my dress up and pulled him inside with me. My Audi wasn’t as spacious in the back as I would have liked, so plans didn’t go as I wanted them to. I leaned down and grabbed his semi-hard erection and started rubbing and massaging the tip trying to get it harder. When that wasn’t happening, we made plans to meet up at his place in an hour. I wanted to go home and freshen up first anyway.

By the time I reached home, I felt guilty for my actions. I couldn't believe I almost had sex with a stranger. Yes, he was a handsome stranger that made me feel things only my husband made me feel. The way he looked at me, made me feel like bending over and pulling him deep inside my kitty. Forty-five minutes passed, and I was still daydreaming about Chance. I shook out of it when my phone chimed with a text from Chance asking if I was, I still coming over. I replied, *no*, and made up a story about feeling sick once I got home.

I hopped in the shower to get comfortable before my soon-to-be-ex-husband arrived home to try and talk his way back into my good graces. In the shower I fell into a deep gaze as the hot water hit my body. I thought of all the times Jonah didn't come home or stayed at work until close. It hit me like a ton of bricks, and I suddenly felt sick. I ran over to the toilet at the nick of time! The feelings in my stomach had me all kinds of nauseous. I dried off and laid down. I must have fell asleep because when I woke the clock read 12:05 am and Jonah still wasn't home. I snatched the covers up, turned over, and went back to bed.

Hours later I was awakened by a tug on my arm, “Baby can we talk?” I laid there still as ever making sure he didn’t see me flinch, as I pretended to be sleep. Jonah tugged away at my arm trying to get my attention as I just laid there. He finally gave up, turned over and went to sleep.

The next morning, I woke up to the aroma of salmon croquettes. As I got out of bed my body slipped from under me and I yelled as I dropped to the floor. My head was spinning, and I tried to get up, but my legs wouldn’t move. Jonah must’ve heard me because he rushed in and asked if I was alright as he attempted to help me. I couldn't move. He picked me up, quickly checked my pulse, and when he noticed I wasn’t breathing, he rushed me out of the house and into the car.

Jonah

I woke up early to surprise Neveah with breakfast in bed. I decided to cook her favorite salmon croquettes, cheese grits, French toast, and cheese eggs. Suddenly, I heard a loud noise, *Boooooooom!!*

“Neveah! Neveah!!” When I didn’t hear her respond, I turned off the stove and ran to the bedroom. I was in shock! Seeing Neveah there, laid on the floor, I panicked! I rushed over to her side of the bed and tried to get her to stand, but she was too weak. I picked her up and tried to check her pulse. Her breaths were faint but steady, so I rushed her out to the car to take her to the hospital.

“Somebody HELPPPPP MEEEE. My wife needs attention! HELPPPPP!” I yelled as I rushed through the hospital doors, carrying Neveah in my arms. Nurses ran towards me with a stretcher asking *what happened*. I recapped the events as they transferred her off the stretcher to the bed, put an IV in her arm, and checked her for a concussion.

“Sir, we are going to have to ask you to leave the room for a second while we do a full examination to see what's going on.” I obliged and left. After hours of waiting, the doctor finally came out to talk to me.

“Mr. Jenkins, Sir, Mrs. Jenkins has suffered a head trauma. It's not severe but we would like to keep her overnight for observation. She is awake, but she is very weak from the fall. The good thing is, both her and the baby will be fine.”

My heart dropped. “Baby? Did you say baby?”

“Yes, Mrs. Jenkins is 16 weeks pregnant. Were you both unaware?” she asked confused.

“I didn’t know, and I'm not sure if she did. But thanks so much Dr. Can I go back and see her now?” I asked.

“Sure, just try and keep her relaxed Mr. Jenkins. The baby doesn’t need any stress.” I thanked him and walked back to the room Neveah was in. I knocked and walked in. There she was rubbing her belly and smiling so hard you could see all her teeth. I didn’t know whether to be happy or sad about bringing a child into this now broken marriage.

“Did you hear the news?” she gleamed.

“Yes, I did, but why didn’t you tell me you were pregnant?”

“I just found out, but this couldn't have come at a better time.”

“How could you say that Neveah with all the things we have going on?”

“Jonah, what you did is done. We will get a divorce and you can still see your child,” Neveah said while still rubbing her belly. “I could never hate this baby; I could never give this baby up just because you’re a lying dog.”

“Neveah, I want to make this work, I promise you nothing like this will happen again,” I said with all sincerity. But Neveah wasn’t buying it.

"Honestly Jonah, I could have taken you back despite walking in and seeing you get topped by some random thot! But the fact that you have been having an affair for months and got the thirsty bitch pregnant, and that thirst bucket had the audacity to come up to my job and blind side me to tell me… Nah, there is nothing you can say that would convince me to stay with you after all that mess. There is nothing you can do or say."

After she uttered those words, what could I say? I turned around and headed for the nearest exit.

Neveah

The nerve this man has, thinking we could ever be anything besides co-parents is beyond me. Getting the news that I was pregnant was the best news I received in a while. Jonah and I had been trying for months. Now, it's finally happening. I wasn't going to let nothing or no one stress me to the point of harming my baby, so this so-called marriage that my husband stepped out on is officially over.

They ran tests to make sure that me and the baby were okay and not at risk from any underlying health concerns. The doctor released me after a few days. I was so anxious to get back to my routine and my clients at work. Psychiatry is my passion, the happiness I get from helping people through the toughest times of their lives gives me a joy indescribable. I'm thrilled to help people cope with all their trials and tribulations. I hurried home and prepared for work.

"Welcome back Ms. Jenkins!" Porsha yelled as she ran up to me with her hands out. "Thanks Porsha," I smiled and motioned for her to follow me into my office. I noticed someone sitting with their back to me in the dark. I switched the light on, "Ummmm, hello how can I help you this afternoon Miss?" I asked with hesitation.

The woman stood up and turned around with a sinister smile on her face, arms folded.

“What the hell are you doing in my office?” I asked, trying to remain calm.

I reached over and grabbed the phone from my desk and called security. The audacity of this woman standing in my office waiting for me to arrive has my attitude on 10. Before I could speak, Julia snatched the phone from my ear and hung it up.

“Ma’am, please leave my office now while I am allowing you to leave. Otherwise, I will call the police and have you escorted out of my office.”

She stood without a move, as if I hadn’t said a word. She began to burst out laughing. Porsha walked over and pled with her to leave. But when she saw that she wasn’t budging scurried out of my office to get security. I couldn't hold my emotions any longer. I was done with this woman! I grabbed her arm and pushed her out of my office and closed my door. She tried to force the door open but once she saw it was locked, she left.

Thirty minutes later there was a firm knock at the door. Julia walked in accompanying two police officers. I chuckled softly.

“Ma’am I assume you already know why we are here. But why don’t you tell us what happened?” The chunky officer asked.

“Nothing happened really. I came in and that woman was in my office. I asked her to leave, and she refused. I helped her out by grabbing her arm and walking her to the door. Why she called you here, I have no idea! She is the home-wrecker sleeping with my husband, and I don’t want her anywhere near me or my unborn child,” I said looking for Julia’s reaction.

I must have hit her with a ton of bricks because her face squirmed, and she stormed off in a rage. The officers yelled out to Julia, “Ma’am if you leave, we won’t be able to press charges.” Julia threw her hands up in frustration as she got on the elevator. “Well, Ma’am I'm so sorry for interrupting your day. Obviously, Ms. Strong has left, so no charges will be filed today. Have a nice day."

"Thanks so much," I replied gratefully as the officers left my office.

I walked over to my desk and buzzed Jazmine. "Jazmine what's my schedule look like today?"

"You have a full roster since your absence. Your first appointment just walked in. Once signed in I'll bring them back."

Five minutes later a tall, dark, and handsome Idris Elba looking man walked through the door. "Ms. Jenkins, this is Daniel Keys," Jazmine said as she escorted him.

"Hi Daniel, please have a seat," I said as I extended my hand. Daniel obliged as he smiled and relaxed. "Let's start off with you telling me a little about you and what's troubling you."

Daniel held his head down; I could tell he was struggling with opening up, so I got up and walked over to the couch where he sat and tried to make him more comfortable.

Daniel looked up at me with confusion and sorrow in his eyes. “My wife is cheating on me. I found out two weeks ago when I followed her to his house. He greeted her at the door, and they shared a passionate kiss. I waited for her to leave so that I could confront her, but after two hours I had to leave. I called her ten times, and she never answered.

“After calling and texting her for hours she finally came home. I grilled her about where she had been, and she confessed that she had been cheating on me for months with a guy she met at the grocery store. We haven't said much to one another from that day to this one. But today I went home on my lunch break shocked to find the house completely empty! She took our kid and all of their belongings! I don't know when I'll see my son again,” Daniel said as his mouth trembled.

I felt sorry for Daniel and what he was dealing with. I leaned in to hug him, but somehow our lips touched. I jumped back. Daniel slid his hand up and down my leg and grabbed my waist and attempted to pull me in for a second time. Lost in the trance, I didn't stop him. We kissed passionately as he rubbed my thigh making my kitty purr. I knew this was a bad idea, but I continued to feel this passion, so I wrapped my arms around him tighter. Daniel laid me down and tugged at my dress trying to make his way to my love spot. As he reached closer and closer, I laid there, anticipating, and wanting to feel everything that was coming. He pulled my panties down with his teeth, he kissed and sucked my inner thighs. I was so turned on at this point there was no denying what was about to happen. I lifted and unbuttoned his shirt, unzipped his pants so he could take them off.

We admired the masterpieces in front of us as we kissed and grabbed each other's nude bodies, roughly. I stood up and walked over to the window and sat in the chair that was facing the city, motioning him to follow. I opened my legs as he sat on the floor in front of me. He grabbed my legs and held them in the air as he hungrily tore into my juices. Sweet noises escaped my lips, he reached his hand up and shoved three fingers inside my mouth. I was enjoying every minute of his tongue and then there was a knock on the door shook me from the passion. I jumped up in a frenzy, trying to dress. But he grabbed me and bent me over the chair.

He dived inside me with so much passion and force. I was in full ecstasy. A soft moan slipped from my lips. He bent down, grabbed my panties, and shoved them in my mouth. I was so turned on that I laid down and took every inch while he pushed every inch further inside of my stomach. “Yesss, Daddy! Give it to me! Oooouuu! Fuckkk!” I was on the verge of exploding all my passion on his manhood when he motioned me to get on all fours. I got on my knees instead and hungrily slurped all nine inches of him.

“Ahhh! Ahhh! Oooo!” He screamed as he oozed all over my lips and down my chin. He picked me up and backed me up against the wall. Holding me over his head he licked me all the way until I climaxed.

I chuckled. “What's funny?” Daniel asked smiling. I was in disbelief. Not only was the sex phenomenal, but I just had sex with a stranger, even worse, a client. This had become a trend and I didn’t feel bad about it. I shrugged and smiled.

We rushed to put our clothes on. And it’s a good thing we did because Jazmine briefly knocked before entering, “Ms. Jenkins, your next appointment has arrived.”

“Thank you, Jazmine, I will finish this session up and be right there.” I said through clenched teeth. I was so thankful for the distraction.

“Daniel, I don't think we can see each other on a professional level after this.” I giggled. “I would like to have dinner with you and get to know you. Here is my card with my personal contact information on it. Call me," I said as I walked him out. Not feeling well after this random sexcapade, I had Jazmine reschedule all my appointments for the rest of the day. I needed to go home and clear my head.

Jonah

Neveah's pregnant. I still can't wrap my head around the fact that my marriage is over and her being pregnant makes matters even worse. I love my wife, and the thought of having to see her but not be able to hold and caress her scared me. Despite all the mistakes I made in my marriage, I never thought it would end this way.

Being with other women meant nothing to me, just a craving I had to fill from time to time. My wife was my life, but I couldn't stop wanting more. I must get my wife back. I can't believe Julia went to her job and made a scene. "That bitch gone pay!" I yelled as my phone rang.

Coincidentally it was Julia. Amazed that she had the nerve to call me, I declined the call. She called back-to-back three more times at which point, I finally answered. She just held the phone. “Hellllooo,” my voice echoed in the phone. She still said nothing, so I hung up. I responded with a text asking her to come over and included my location address. We had been screwing for almost a year now, but she didn’t know where I lived. I jumped up and ran in the bathroom as I decided to hop in the shower before she arrived.

While in the shower I heard my phone ringing repeatedly. Something had to be wrong, so I jumped out, grabbed a towel, and hurried to see who called. I was shocked to see three messages from Neveah telling me she was outside and needed to talk. As I dried off, I noticed two texts from Julia telling me she would be on her way soon. I hurried and called Julia in an attempt to tell her not to stop by. She didn’t pick up. So, I texted her saying I felt queasy, and we would have to meet another time. I hurried to the door to let my wife in. “What was taking you so long? I almost left!" Neveah said.

I didn't even respond. I just grabbed her hand to pull her in. I helped her out of her coat and directed her to the bedroom. I was surprised that she stopped at the dining room table and dropped her purse. I took it as a sign that she didn't want to go any further. This wasn't a "let's chill" visit.

"I only came to have a discussion about our baby, and to discuss how we will be moving forward." Neveah said seriously.

"Neveah, baby I miss you so much. Please come home and let's talk about this. I know I messed up and stepped out on this marriage but you're my wife and I can't lose you. Those women meant nothing to me, you're the woman I love, the mother of my unborn child and I want to make this marriage work if you are willing to," I grabbed Neveah's hand to show her I was sincere.

The knock on the door caught both of our attention. With the knock at the door came a ring on my phone. I ignored it and didn't even look to see who was calling.

"Let me in Jonah! I know you're in there." I got up and rushed to address the problem at the door. I tried to calm Julia down and get her to be quiet, but she wasn't having it.

Again, with the nonstop ringing on my phone. Who is blowing my phone up right now? I didn't have time for this.

I pushed Julia outside and pulled the front door behind me. "Why are you here Julia? I know you saw my text!"

"Of course, I saw your damn text Jonah, but I'm not thinking about what you want, and obviously you ain't sick! You busy over here with that Bitch! What the hell is she doing here?"

"Imma need you to stop referring to her as a bitch."

"Bitch, bitch, bitch," she sang.

“Calm down and let’s talk right now.”

I couldn’t take the ringing of my phone. I looked down and saw there were three missed calls from Kimberly. This must be bitch-lose-your-mind-day. What could she want? “What up Kimberly?”

Neveah

I couldn’t believe what I was hearing. The thot that visited my office was now here. I could tell Jonah was trying to calm her down, but it wasn’t working. Not to mention, she called me out of my name one to many times. It was time for me to leave. I didn’t need to put myself or my baby at risk. I grabbed my bag and headed for the door.

As I was headed out Julia was headed in. “Where you going bitch? Oh, you ready to leave now, huh?! Well, we need to have some words!” Julia stormed passed me as she swung her coat off and tossed it on the chair.

"I have nothing to say to you," I said as I walked past Julia. Well, at least I thought I walked past her. She must've stuck her foot out because the next thing you know, *Booommm!!!* I was on the ground. I can't believe this thot tripped me.

I was shocked by the fall and tried to gain my composure, but Julia was out for blood! She came to fight. She grabbed my hair, flipped me over. I attempted to cover my face as I saw her heel headed towards it. But when she couldn't kick my face, she kicked my stomach. When she couldn't kick my stomach, she stomped my face

I couldn't do much. I felt frozen because all I could think about was protecting my baby. Then, I thought, *where the hell is Jonah?*

The pain was excruciating as she kicked and stomped me repeatedly. When I tried to get up, Julia knocked me back down. "Helppp!!!" was all I could utter.

Jonah

"What's so urgent that you gotta be blowing my phone up like this?"

"I'll tell you what's urgent. Me wanting some more of what you gave me," Kimberly purred.

"Kimberly, not right now. I have to get back to you. I've got an emergency and," *Booommm!* I heard a loud noise.

"But baby," Kimberly pled, "I need you right now."

"Kimberly, look, we'll connect later! I gotta handle this!" I yelled.

I heard Neveah calling out for help. I couldn't believe what I saw! I rushed in grabbed Julia and threw her off of Neveah causing her to crash into the chair and fall.

"Neveah, baby, are you okay?" I asked as I tried to help her up. She was in pain, and it was written all over her face. "Oooooo," she groaned as she tried to move her bloody body.

I was so fucking angry with Julia! I bum-rushed her and threw her into the wall. Her body dropped and I began to kick her repeatedly until her body went still. Her chest beatless, her face began to turn pale. I looked over at Neveah. The entire time as she was screaming and begging me to stop.

Neveah grabbed her keys and mustered up all the strength she had left and headed for the door.

Deranged, I ran over and stopped her in her tracks. Neveah was frightened, bloody, and shaky. She tried to move past me, but I wouldn't let her pass. "You ain't seen nothing! Keep this out your mouth!" I spat. Speechless, she just nodded her head letting me know she understood. I moved out of her way and Neveah rushed to her car.

Julia

When I received that message from Jonah, my heart melted. He finally invited me over for a night cap. I jumped up, took a shower, and threw on something extra sexy. I picked up my phone to put the address in my GPS. I pulled out my driveway, excited about the thought of seeing Jonah when I noticed a text from him saying he suddenly didn't feel well. I didn't care, I was dressed and ready to go see my man. I pulled up to the address and was surprised to see this bitch's car in the driveway, the same car I saw at her office the day I went to confront her about her husband. I instantly grew pissed. He called me over here and she's here!

I jumped out of the car and hurried to the door. Jonah met me at the door trying to calm me down. But I wasn't having that. I needed to put Neveah in her place. And since Jonah was distracted by a phone call, this was my time to have some words with Neveah.

I moved past him, entered his house, and threw my coat on the chair. She uttered some words that instantly set me off and had the nerve to walk off all dismissively. I was livid, she was not about to disrespect me. As she walked toward the exit, I stuck my foot out in hopes of making her fall. The fact that she was carrying his baby and he wanted me to get rid of mine infuriated me. To my amusement she hit the ground and I started wailing on her. I wanted to make her feel the way Jonah has made me feel for the past month about our relationship.

I blacked out. I'm not sure how long I was out, but when I returned to reality, I felt my body release from the floor. Jonah threw me off her. I hit my head and was unaware for a second until I felt Jonah kicking me. The pain intensity was unbearable. I couldn't take it anymore. I could feel my body going numb. It was at that moment I realized I wasn't going to make it out of this house. I began to pray for forgiveness and mercy. A tear rolled down my cheek. *Booom!* That was the stomp that took my last breath.

I no longer felt anything.

Neveah

I cannot believe what I just witnessed. The man that I love just killed a pregnant woman right in front of me. "Ooouuu!" I screamed in agony. I focused and finally made it to the hospital. I was in so much pain, that I knew something had to be wrong with my baby. They ran test after test as I prayed for a miracle. More than anything, I wanted my baby to be okay. Saddened and startled by the events that occurred, I broke down. I needed to talk to somebody, anybody.

I reached for my phone and sent a text. I needed to see a familiar face. "I need to see you. Please come to Mercy Hospital emergency room."

An hour later Chance came rushing in with a concerned look on his face. I was so emotional that I just broke down. He hurried to console me. "What happened Neveah? What are you doing here?" Chance asked.

Embarrassed by the truth, I looked away and wept softly. "I'm pregnant."

I continued, “I'm married, my husband and I are in a bad place. I'm looking to get a divorce, but I want to keep this baby. I am so lost and don’t know what to do.” I was shaking. Chance grabbed me and pulled me in closer. Tears flowed uncontrollably. I couldn’t believe how messed up my life had become.

“I have to go to the bathroom; I'll be right back,” Chance said as he got up and headed for the door. It was odd because he said it so suddenly. But I did just drop a lot of information on him, I’m sure it confused him. After twenty minutes I realized he wasn’t back and tried to call him. “The person you are trying to reach has a voicemail that has not been set up yet.” He sent me to voicemail. I felt alone, and the tears started to flow again. I laid there soaking in my sorrows and drifted off to sleep.

Chance

Buzzz, my phone vibrated in my pocket as I left the hospital to my car. It was Neveah, I felt bad, but I had to get out of there. She is a beautiful woman but broken. I just wanted a good time. I would have been there to listen but wasn't prepared for a husband and a baby on the way. Get out while I can seemed to be the only sensible thing to do.

A text coming through my Car Play speaker caught my attention. "The package will be dropped off at 1 am @ the spot. Don't be late." This threw me off because it was already 12:45 am. I sped off. By the time I reached the spot I saw blue lights. I didn't know what was going on so as I got closer, I stopped and parked. I called the number that texted me. No one answered, which never happened. I was nervous. It wasn't like my brother to not answer the phone.

A second later sirens blared. The ambulance was racing past me to the address I was headed. After about five minutes the paramedics came out with two gurneys, both carrying bodies. Scared to ponder the what-ifs, I jumped out the car and made my way to see what happened.

I was shocked at the sight of my brother laying there lifeless. “What happened, what is going on?” I asked trying to hold my composure while I gathered the facts.

“Nobody knows. We got a call about hearing gunshots and a lot of chaos and when we arrived, nobody was in the house except these two John Does,” the police said appearing suddenly behind me. “Who are you?” The police asked curiously.

“I'm Chance. I live about two streets up. I saw the sirens and wondered what was going on,” I stuttered nervously.

I was so messed up, stunned. I couldn’t believe what was happening. My brother had just texted me and now he’s dead. If I had been here like I was supposed to then maybe I could have prevented this. Tears started to stream down my face, but I wasn’t about to make this moment any worse than it already was. At that moment I knew life was about to change. I rushed to my car, I knew I had to go over and talk with my mom and dad before they saw it on the news or heard it from someone else.

Jonah

Getting rid of Julia's body was too much for me tonight, I was so wound up and needed to lay down and calm my nerves. I walked upstairs, turned on the shower and began to undress. I had just killed her with my bare hands in front of Neveah. At that moment, as my adrenaline slowed, I realized that I had lost my wife for sure now. Neveah would never get over what just happened. It was no coming back from this fuck up. Julia got what she deserved and for that I wasn't at all sorry for ending her. I finished my shower and headed to bed.

The next morning, I woke up eager to get this body out my life. I called my cousin Vinny for help. When he arrived, he was in disbelief at the scene he walked into. Blood was everywhere. We grabbed the rug next to Julia's body and used it to roll her up inside. My cousin grabbed the bleach and ammonia and started wiping down the house from top to bottom. I had to get to work, so I left the cleaning to him and trusted him to be discreet and discard all evidence.

I arrived at work to find Keisha in my office. She was naked sitting at my desk waiting for me. I hadn't seen her in days, she called off and didn't show up for work for almost a week, so I was wondering what the hell she was doing here.

“Keisha what are you doing in my office? I don't have time for this today,” I said. Keisha didn't answer she just got up and walked over to me and rubbed her body against mine letting me know exactly what she wanted. Keisha was a stripper I hired way back. I knew her from the old neighborhood. She was gorgeous, 5'8”, with a dark chocolate slim body, medium and oh-so-perky breasts, and a slim, juicy Georgia peach-shaped booty that I never could stay away from. One of the first strippers I hired when Truth first opened, we messed around soon after she started. We would mess around every day when I arrived at work and again before I headed home.

Then she got engaged to one of her regulars and all that changed. We still messed around, but not as much. I started messing with Julia, Keisha got jealous and started throwing it at me every chance she got.

Today was one of those days she wanted it. She pushed me against the desk chair knocking me back into reality. She tried to unzip my pants, but I stopped her. “Keisha, I have a lot of work to do today. I'm not in the mood, I have too much work to do.”

I motioned her to leave my office, but she didn’t listen. She sat down on top of me and attempted to kiss me. I was so annoyed. Today was not the day! I pushed her off me, flew the door open for her to leave. She sat at my desk, grabbed her purse, and started fumbling around. “Keisha, leave before I have security come and remove you,” I huffed. Keisha continued to put on her lipstick.

I was pissed now, instead of calling security I walked over and grabbed her but to my surprise she snatched away from me dropping her purse in the midst. I picked up her purse, headed towards the door to toss it out. Keisha ran behind me and tried to take it, I opened the door tossed the purse out and tried to push her out with it. Keisha wasn't budging.

I grabbed my desk phone, "Someone please come up and escort Ms. Greene off the premises." A few seconds later two security guards entered. "How can we help you?" the guard asked as he glanced around the office. "Yes, please escort Ms. Greene out of my office and out of my club. Oh yeah, and Keisha, you're fired!" I said with a smirk. "Gentleman please take her key card. She won't need to access my club anymore."

"Yes sir."

Neveah

I woke ups to the noises from the machines hooked up to my body. I couldn't believe how terrible my life had become. I was at an all-time low. I needed my husband. I wanted my husband. I would do anything for this nightmare to end. Just a few weeks ago I was happy and in bliss and today I'm pregnant, unhappy, and thinking of getting a divorce. This is not what I want for my baby. A household with no father. I always wanted to be a mother, but never imagined being a single mother trying to co-parent with my ex-husband that had an affair and killed the side chick in front of me. I cried. The doctor entered and I dried my face quickly.

“Ms. Jenkins your little one is doing fine, and we patched you up so now we can release you,” she said with a slight smile. “You must take it easy. No more foul play.”

“Yes, Doctor, of course,” I smiled. I was ready to get out of this hospital and get home. I got up, changed into my clothes, and drove home.

When I arrived, I noticed a red Subaru parked by my mailbox. I exited my car and walked toward my front door when the driver stepped out. I unlocked my door to go in when Daniel grabbed my hand. Shocked that he even knew where I lived, I shoved past him to get in the house.

"Daniel what are you doing here?" I asked.

"I wanted to talk to you, I went to your office, and they said you weren't in today, so I came over hoping you were home. I haven't been able to get you out of my head since the last time we were together," Daniel smiled.

I felt uneasy and annoyed. "Daniel how did you find out where I live? We haven't spoken since our last session. Why would you just drop by my house?"

Daniel walked closer without hesitation. "I need to feel you. Everywhere I go I smell you. I crave your touch and want to feel your body under mine. I can't stop thinking about slowly going in and out that sweet, wet, shaved peach until you climax all over me."

He was turning me on, but given the day I had, I was in no mood to entertain his advances, so I asked him to leave. But he wasn't trying to leave.

"Neveah please understand that I love you. You are all I think about. I want you. I cannot go back home without you," he said.

"Daniel I'm married!" I screamed. "I don't want to do this with you right now. I'm just getting home from the hospital, I'm really tired, and I need to take a shower and rest. So, if you don't mind, please LEAVE!" I shouted.

Daniel just stood there with a blank face. I unlocked my door and entered. I didn't have time for this.
Daniel pushed me inside my house, grabbed me, and pushed me against the wall. He rubbed his fingers across my thighs which instantly made me leak. He got excited and picked me up. I stopped fighting and started kissing him. Daniel returned the kisses holding me tightly.

He walked us over to the kitchen counter. I laid down as Daniel locked and sucked all those fluids that poured freely down my caramel thighs. I jumped and bucked as Daniel gave me the best tongue I experienced in a while. I could not hold back, I squirted all over his beard and mouth. I jumped down, as he stood there hard as a rock. I pulled up a chair and pushed him down. I started twerking on top of him. I wanted to make him beg for me. He pulled me down and grabbed my head and guided me to his hard on. I put all of him inside my mouth. He groaned. I sucked Daniel so good he started to pre cum almost instantly. I then climbed on top. He grabbed my waist as I rode him like it was no tomorrow. He must've felt himself about to release, but wasn't ready, so he picked me up and pressed me against the counter. He got behind me and bent me all the way over making me grab my ankles as he pounded me from the back hard. "Ooouuu, yessss Daniel! Give it to me!" I screamed.

Daniel was so turned on and amped up he picked me up and spread my legs on the counter. From the back he inserted inside my wetness again. I had never felt so much passion, he was driving in and out of me with so much ecstasy and force. I was on the verge of erupting. I got down on my knees and slurped him into submission. "Dammmnnn," Daniel moaned as he came all in my mouth.

I was exhausted. "Daniel I really need to get some rest now. Can we just talk later?" I asked nicely hoping he would do what I asked and leave. But he was still in bliss; and wasn't ready to leave.

"That was great! Why do I have to leave Neveah?" he asked confused.

"I need to take a shower and get some rest," I said.

"Can I get in the shower with you?" he smiled.

"No, Daniel, I need to be alone!" I screamed. I was getting so annoyed at this point. He must've heard the annoyance in my voice because he finally decided to listen.

“I'll leave. But I'll be back Neveah. We got to finish what we started. I love you,” he said smiling as he walked toward the door.

He had me so confused with his feelings. Obviously, I just slept with a highly delusional guy. Yes, we had good sex twice, but that’s all it was: good sex. I felt no connection whatsoever to this man and here he is saying he loves me. I had to get out of my head and stop analyzing. I went to shower and finally laid down to get that rest I desperately needed.

Chance

I didn’t know what to tell my parents. Chris was their everything. He was the youngest and the child that could do no wrong. I was hurt and could not believe someone killed my brother. To make matters worse, I had to tell my parents before they heard it elsewhere.

I reached my parents' house at 2:16 am. It took everything in me to unlock that door and enter. I only wish I would have arrived at his home just a few moments earlier. But what's done is done. I knocked on my parent's room door, I got no answer. Knock, knock, knock I continued to knock, but still, there was no answer. I walked in but wasn't ready to see what was before me. There lay mom and dad on the floor with blood everywhere. I felt broken and numb. My parents laid there, butchered to death.

I called 911. As I waited, I sat crying, freaking out, and beating myself up. "Why the fuck is this happening?" I yelled as I started pacing. "Who the fuck did this?" My tears turned into anger. I wanted blood. This was no coincidence; someone targeted my family. I grabbed my phone and scrolled through the contact list. I found the contact I was looking for, called the number, and my call went straight to voicemail. I called again and again until I got an answer.

"Hello," I heard the raspy voice say. "Meet me at 22nd and 1st street in 30 minutes," he said and hung up. I sobbed for a few more minutes. I said my goodbyes, kissed mom on the forehead and grabbed dad's hand. I was on a mission. I left and made my way to meet the voice on the other end of the phone.

When I arrived, I noticed the black Jaguar sitting off in the cut beside the dumpster. I exited the car and walked over to the Jaguar. I leaned down as the door opened and the driver got out. *Bammm!* I punched him in the jaw, he fell to the ground, and I punched him again and again. I was filled with so much anger and had lost it. Once I snapped back to reality, I picked him up and carried him to my car. I needed answers! He appeared to be unconscious, so I grabbed the water out my trunk and threw it in his face to wake him.

"So, you killed my family tonight? You shot my fucking parents!!" I screamed. "They had nothing to do with this and you damn shoot them!" I started wailing on him again. "You killed my brother!" He just sat there taking hit after hit. I pulled my gun out about to end him when a thump in the back of my head saved his life. I fell to the ground, and everything went black.

Jonah

This hoe Keisha has really pissed me off. Coming in here with her married ass trying to make me sleep with her. She was looking sexy, but I just had too much on my mind. I must figure out how I'm going to get my wife back. I wasn't ready to lose her. I want to be in my baby's life. I want to be a full-time father. I just didn't know what to do.

Knock Knock…Come in I said. Gloria is a freak from way back. She used to date my best friend in college, and I dated her sister. We became friends and I gave her a job when I first opened. She wanted to be one of my main girls. We slept together once, and she instantly started avoiding me. She only came to see me when she had a problem. Gloria entered and sat down.

"What can I do for you Gloria?" I asked.

“I need an advance and time off,” Gloria said with her head down and a sad face.

“What's going on?”

“My mom is in the hospital, and I need to go to Dallas to be with her. I don’t know when I will be back, but I don’t want to leave and have no job to return to.”

“Of course, take all the time you need, make sure mom's okay,” I said in a supportive tone. “Your job will be here when you come back,” I assured her.

“Thank you so much.” Gloria got up and walked over to the desk and kissed me on the cheek. I moved my face and kissed her on the lips. She didn’t pull back. I grabbed her face and kissed her passionately. Gloria stopped, looked at me and rushed towards the door. “See you when I get back,” she said as she shut the door behind her. I could not help myself; I was not in the mood, but I liked the chase that came with Gloria.

My phone rang. It was the devil. I dismissed the call. He left a voicemail. “When you get this message, you better call me back or you will come home to a dead wife and cat!” You have 20 minutes and I'll be headed to your house to kill everything moving!” the voice screamed.

I immediately called back. I didn't even want to see if he was joking or not. The phone rang once, “Hello,” the man said.

“If anything happens to my wife, your whole family is dead,” I said with aggression.

“You better get my package to me by the end of the day, or your family is dead,” The voice said remaining calm and unphased by my threat.

“If you call me again threatening me, you’re going to see the real deadly side of me, and your family will be dead!” I screamed.

The man laughed with no worry in his voice. I was annoyed. “I'll be coming by later to make the drop, but it will be at the warehouse on 23rd and Bainbridge this time."

"I'll send my associate to do the drop off. Don't be 20 cents short or my next stop will be Truth and you won't see another day."

The call disconnected. I had been dabbling in a lot more than entertainment lately, and it was costing me everything.

Neveah

I woke up the next morning and was still at a lost as to how Daniel could love me. We do not even know each other. I was interrupted by a knock on the window. Startled I rushed to grab my robe to check it out. Flabbergasted at the sight of seeing Daniel standing there smiling and waving for me to open the window, I rolled my eyes and closed my curtains.

I walked towards the bathroom in hopes he got the message and left. The phone rang, and Daniel's name popped up. I did not answer. He called back-to-back, leaving voicemail after voicemail. I could not take it anymore and sent a text that read: *Daniel I don't know what you are doing here but I didn't invite you here and you can't just show up to my house without permission. I must get ready for work, and I wish you would stop calling me.*

I silenced the ringer and laid the phone on the counter. Despite my morning starting off crazy I could not wait to get to work. I danced in front of the mirror for a moment then ran to the closet to get clothes out and rushed in the shower. I was already running behind.

Thirty minutes later I was dressed and ready to go. I walked out the house and noticed Daniel's car still parked outside. I shook my head in aggravation. I walked to the car as Daniel jumped out trying to reach me before I got in.

"I need to talk to you," Daniel pleaded as I walked faster. I got in and began adjusting the seat belt to leave. Daniel got upset, he grabbed my arm through the window and squeezed.

“Do you think you can just sleep with me and ignore me?” Daniel snapped.

“Daniel if you don’t let me go and leave my house, I will be calling the police!” I yelled while snatching my arm and shutting the door.

I was late for work and Daniel was beginning to make me angry. Daniel wouldn’t budge he just stood there looking. I backed out and sped off. As I reached the end of the street, I realized that Daniel had gotten in his car and was coming behind me at a fast speed. This guy is acting crazy. I sped up in hopes of him leaving me alone.

By the time I reached work it was 11 am. I walked in and was greeted by my assistant and client that was already waiting for me. I went into my office and prepared for my next session. Ten minutes later in walked Jazmine and my client.

“Ms. Jenkins this is Ms. Jacks.”

“Thanks Jazmine. Hello Ms. Jacks, how are you today?”

“I’m fine, thanks so much for asking.”

“What brings you in today?” I said as I got out pen and paper.

Ms. Jacks reached into her purse and pulled out a piece of paper, I was puzzled. With all the surprises happening lately I didn’t know what to expect. Ms. Jacks started to cry. “My husband asked me for a divorce. I don’t know how things got so messed up. We were just madly in love and then he started to act different. I noticed and asked him to get counseling, but he laughed at the idea. A couple of days later I went through his phone and saw naked pictures of a random woman.

“I confronted him and he left, and I haven’t seen him since. I was served with divorce papers this morning. I called him. But he didn’t answer so I went over to his brother’s house where I figured he would be. I pulled up to the house and boom, there he was coming out the house with another woman. I was so angry I went over and made a huge scene.

“It resulted in the police being called and me being escorted off the premises. I am at a loss for words. I cannot believe the man that I love could be capable of this type of disrespect. I want to sign these papers but every time I pick up the pen, my hands freeze. This man has always loved and cared for me, but this morning he showed just how much he no longer cares.

“I haven’t been able to sleep, and I feel like I am losing my mind. It’s been 3 days since I got any sleep. I need something doc to help me calm down. I feel myself slowly breaking down.”

I was at lost for words. I am going through something similar and was not over the hurt from it, so I sympathized with her.

“Ms. Jacks I am so sorry that this is happening to you. I know this is a challenging time for you, but I want you to know that this isn’t your fault. Sometimes things just don’t work out even when we want them to. I want to do an exercise with you. Close your eyes, lay back and rest your mind and body. Take your mind and your thoughts to your happy place. Imagine a place that makes you happy. Think of something that makes you happy. Where are you?”

“On the beach, me and my son playing volleyball,” she smiled.

“Lay in the sand, feel the breeze swift through your hair. Sand underneath your toes, the calming, relaxing sound of the ocean. Are you at peace?” I asked while humming softly.

She didn’t respond. “Ms. Jacks, are you at peace?” I asked once more before getting up to walk over and see what was happening. Ms. Jacks was sleeping. I chuckled before waking her.

"Well, I see that worked as I hoped it would. Ms. Jacks this situation that you are dealing with is certainly stressful for you. But the good thing is sometimes if we block out the world just for a moment and go to our happy place that calms us and releases a lot of that backed up aggression.

"The exercise we just did puts you to sleep which means you let go of all the stress and anxiety you were holding. It allowed your body to relax. I am going to give you something for the anxiety and anxiousness. I want you to take these for a couple of days and monitor yourself. If you still feel the anxiety after a week, I want you to come back and see me and we will try something else. Don't take this medicine but once a day and do not consume any alcoholic beverages or it could have major side effects. I hope this helps and I want to see you back in about two weeks for a follow up visit." I handed her the prescription, and she was on her way.

Daniel

I can't believe how she is treating me. I told her I loved her, and she didn’t even say it back. I thought we had a connection, but it seems like she has just been using me! After showing up to her house and then following Neveah to her job, I was hell bent on speaking to her and making sure she understood how much I loved her. I did not want to go into her office, so I pulled out my phone and called.

“Hello, I'm here to see Neveah.”

“She isn't available, may I take a message?”

“No, I need to speak to Neveah it's an emergency.”

“Okay. May I ask who’s calling so I can let her know?”

“It’s Daniel. Would you please put her on the phone?”

“One moment.”

After a few minutes she came back to the phone. “Ms. Jenkins is not available right now and she will be busy the rest of the day. Please leave your number and I'll give it to her.”

I hung up, got out of the car, and made my way inside. As soon as I walked in, I noticed the girl behind the desk looking at me funny. She must have recognized me from the last time I was here. “Hi, how may I help you?” she asked.

“I am here to see Neveah.”

“Ms. Jenkins is not available. I thought I told you that when you called Sir. She will be busy for the remainder of the day.”

I huffed as I was getting annoyed. “I need to see Neveah and I am not leaving until I see her!”

She stood up and pressed the button notifying security. “Sir, I am going to have to ask you to leave! Ms. Jenkins is not available. She is in with a client and cannot stop what she is doing. You can leave a number and message and I will give it to her, that is all I can do at this moment."

She attempted to rectify the situation as she waited for security. But I was not leaving, I continued to stand and demand to see Neveah when security showed up.

"Hey Jazmine. What's going on here?" security asked.

"Hey guys I've asked him to leave but he won't, he is demanding to see Ms. Jenkins but she is busy and cannot be disturbed. Would you guys make him leave?" Jasmine asked.

"Okay sir we are going to have to escort you off the premises," security said while motioning for me to walk with them. I stood firm and asked for Neveah again.

"Sir, if you don't leave, we will have to call the police," one of the security guards stated. I did not care and headed towards

Neveah's office as I heard Jazmine calling the police. I froze, walked over to Jazmine, and yanked the phone from her. I was pissed! I slapped Jazmine and threw the phone on the floor.

Security grabbed me and forced me to the floor as the other called the police. I was kicking and yelling.

"Neveah…Neveah…Neveah… I need to talk to you!" Five minutes later the police arrived. Jazmine was distraught and she looked like she wanted to kill me.

"What happened here?" The police asked. Security responded, "We were called up here for this guy because he wouldn't leave after being told that Ms. Jenkins was busy and wouldn't be available for the rest of the day. She asked him to leave he refused. So, he marched over to Neveah's door. Jazmine started to call the police and he slapped her and broke her phone. We had to subdue him to get him to calm down."

“Ma’am are you wanting to press charges?” the police asked. Jazmine did not speak.

I started screaming again. “Neveah, Neveah I need to speak to you!” I yelled

“Sir I'm going to need you to lower your voice,” The officer said. I continued to scream. The officer grabbed me and escorted me out. The other officer stayed back to finish taking a statement. As I was being escorted out, I heard the officer asking Jazmine again if she wanted to press charges. I didn’t hear her response. All I heard was the officer say, “Okay then Ma’am, I'm going to leave my card right here in case you change your mind.”

Chance

When I woke up, I didn’t know where I was or what happened. Last thing I remembered was driving to meet Julio on 22nd and 1st. Memories returned, as I thought of my parents being gone. I grew angry, I tried to move and that's when I realized I was tied up. I wiggled and tried to untie the knots holding my hands. I heard footsteps behind me. “Save your strength, you may need it later,” the voice said with a chuckle.

I recognized the voice immediately. It was the same voice that I vowed to kill the next time I saw him. Being in the game brings you enemies you didn’t even mean to acquire. My brother wasn't built for this life, but it drew him in anyway. My brother admired all the perks and power being in the game gave you. He didn’t realize that where there is power there is also pain, and that's where I am right now.

My brother and my parents getting killed wasn’t a coincidence. My brother crossed these people and paid for it with his life and my parents’ lives. *Booop!* A blow to the head woke me out my thoughts.

“A week ago, we got our drop and noticed that it was a little lighter than normal. Where the hell is my money?” he yelled as he threw another punch, but this time in my rib cage.

“Awwhh,” I yelled out in agony. “I don’t know what you are talking about,” I said trying to speak with shallow breaths. He grew angry.

“I'm going to ask you one more time and then things are going to get really dark for you and everyone else you love!” The man said with a tone that even I knew was not a game.

I giggled. “You already killed my brother, my mom and my dad. That was my fucking family!” I said growing angrier by the moment.

“Indeed, I did,” he said with a slight chuckle that made my flesh crawl. “We have been following you for a week now and noticed you with this light skinned beauty. Maybe she is a reason to tell me where my money is!”

I was confused, and then it hit me who he was referring to. I began to sweat; “She has nothing to do with this. She doesn’t even know me. I was hired as her bodyguard for a couple of days," I said nervously. I could not believe that I was being followed and didn't even know it. Neveah was in danger, and I couldn't do anything about it. I grew wary. I pulled at the rope in an effort to unravel it and get away. The man laughed harder and harder. He got up walked into the darkness until he was on the other side of the door. I was worried. Neveah was pregnant, alone, and the worst part about it all was that she had nothing to do with this.

Struggling with the rope was a bust, the ropes were not budging. After several unsuccessful attempts, I remembered I always kept my spare phone in my back pocket. I tried to reach my pocket and luckily the phone was still there. After a few tries I managed to grab the top and pull it out. With my hands tied behind my back. I did all I could to redial any number from my speed dial. The phone started ringing.

Just as someone answered, the door opened. "Hello," I heard Neveah pick up the phone. He ran over and took the phone before I could warn her of the danger that I had exposed her to. “Hellloooo…” I heard coming from the phone.

“NEVEAH LEAVE!” I managed to scream before the phone disconnected. “Shit!” the guy cursed while panicking. He checked my pockets before he brought me in, but he did not know of the backup phone I had. His boss was going to be pissed.

He paced back and forth trying to figure out how he could fix the mess he just created before his boss got a whiff of it and all hell broke loose. I laughed loud, I could tell the man was nervous and worried which gave me leverage to use against him.

“You may as well let me go She will know something is wrong and track my location. I called my people before I called her. They’ve already tracked my location and will be here in the next couple of minutes. If you let me go and leave now, then maybe you can get away before you die right here for nothing,” I said trying to get into his head.

The guy smirked. *Powwow!!* That was the last breath I took as the gunman shot me point blank range in my head.

Neveah

I couldn't believe the mess Daniel caused. Coming up to my place of business, causing a scene and hitting my assistant, not to mention he keeps showing up at my house. I have got to get a restraining order to keep him away from me. If I knew sleeping with him would do this, I would have never done it.

Today was getting longer and longer. I was headed to my doctor's appointment when my phone rang. The number was unfamiliar, but I answered anyway. "Hello," I said as I put the key in the ignition. There was no response. "Hellllooo," I said getting aggravated. "NEVEAH LEAVE!!" was all I heard before the line went dead.

I tried calling back but there was no answer. The more the voice played over and over in my head I realized that it sounded like Chance. I tried calling again but no answer. I didn't know what was going on. I didn't know for sure if it was Chance, but he wasn't answering. That's when I realized both numbers were almost the same. It was Chance, but what did he mean *leave,* why did the phone disconnect, and now there was no answer? I was beginning to feel uneasy. I didn't know Chance that well, but he seemed like a good guy.

Jonah

Feeling pressured and alone I could not take it anymore. I had made a mockery of my life and did not know where to start to put my life back together. There is no way I can live in the same state as my wife and child and not be a father or a husband. I am lost, lost in my many mistakes but this one I cannot lie my way out of. "There is nothing left here for me." I said as I got on my phone and booked the next flight out to Detroit.

My phone rang abruptly knocking me out of my train of thought. In agony, I gasped at the name that jumped across my phone. In disgust I quickly declined. *What could she want?* I thought to myself. The phone rang again, and the same name appeared.

"What the fuck do you want?" I yelled into the phone.

Keisha spat into the phone, "Nigga you better fix your tone because in seven months your child will!"

Click! I hung up. This bitch got me fucked up I laughed and thought to myself. Little did I know, my life was about to change forever and there was no turning back.

About The Author

Mariah Carson

Mariah Carson is a native of Atlanta, GA. She is a millennial author, who fell in love with the pen at 13 years of age- where it all began. She's a hopeless romantic that loves a happy ending. Her passion and desire yearns for love stories with a twist. Dodging Karma is her premier book of the Love series with more drama to come.